PERCY JACKSON & THE OLYMPIANS

BOOK TWO

THE SEA OF MONSTERS

The Graphic Novel

by

RICK RIORDAN

Adapted by
Robert Venditti

Art by
Attila Futaki

Color by
Tamás Gáspár

Lettering by
Chris Dickey

Disney · HYPERION BOOKS
New York

~GASP!~

PERCY, YOU'RE GOING TO BE LATE!

BE RIGHT THERE!

IT'S ABOUT TIME, *RIP VAN WINKLE.* I THOUGHT YOU'D BE MORE EXCITED.

ONLY *ONE MORE DAY.* YOU'VE ALMOST MADE IT!

LOTS OF KIDS MANAGE TO GO A WHOLE YEAR WITHOUT GETTING EXPELLED FROM SCHOOL, MOM.

ONLY IN *THIS HOUSE* IS IT A CAUSE FOR CELEBRATION.

ALL THE SAME, I *AM* PROUD OF YOU.

BUT IF YOU DON'T FEEL LIKE CELEBRATING, THEN I GUESS AFTER SCHOOL I WON'T TAKE YOU TO THAT *SKATEBOARD STORE* YOU LIKE.

THE SKATE SHOP? *ALL RIGHT!*

WAIT... I THOUGHT AFTER SCHOOL WE WERE GOING TO PACK ME UP FOR **CAMP**.

ABOUT THAT... I GOT A MESSAGE FROM CHIRON LAST NIGHT.

HE SAID IT MIGHT NOT BE... SAFE FOR YOU TO COME TO CAMP JUST YET.

WHAT? HOW COULD IT NOT BE SAFE?

I'M A **HALF-BLOOD**! CAMP IS, LIKE, THE **ONLY** SAFE PLACE ON EARTH FOR ME!

I CAN'T EXPLAIN IT ALL NOW. I'M NOT EVEN SURE I UNDERSTAND EVERYTHING CHIRON TOLD ME.

ALL I KNOW FOR SURE IS HE THINKS WE SHOULD POSTPONE YOUR SUMMER SESSION.

POSTPONE? FOR HOW LONG?

HE DIDN'T SAY. I'M SORRY, PERCY, BUT WE HAVE TO DO WHAT CHIRON THINKS IS BEST.

DOES THIS HAVE ANYTHING TO DO WITH GROVER? I HAD THIS **DREAM**...

I'LL TRY TO FIND OUT MORE, I PROMISE. WE CAN TALK ABOUT IT LATER.

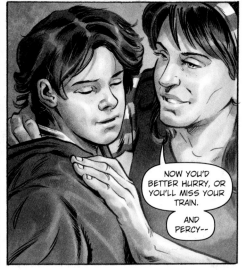

NOW YOU'D BETTER HURRY, OR YOU'LL MISS YOUR TRAIN.

AND PERCY--

"--TRY TO ENJOY YOUR LAST DAY."

WHO IS *THAT*?

MUST BE YOUR COUSIN, BECAUSE THERE'S NO WAY A *HOTTIE* LIKE THAT WOULD BE *YOUR* GIRLFRIEND.

HEY! GIVE BACK MY PHOTO!

I WANTED YOU TO MEET MY *NEW BUDDIES*. THEY'LL ALL BE TRANSFERRING HERE FOR EIGHTH GRADE.

I ALREADY *CAN'T WAIT* FOR NEXT YEAR TO START.

WH--?

YOU LEAVE PERCY ALONE!

AH! LET GO!

TYSON! *PUT HIM DOWN!*

-oof-

YOU'RE SUCH A LOSER, JACKSON. YOU MIGHT ACTUALLY HAVE FRIENDS IF YOU DIDN'T HANG OUT WITH THIS *RETARD.*

HE'S *NOT* RETARDED!

FORGET ABOUT WAITING TILL NEXT YEAR. NEXT *PERIOD* IN P.E.--

--YOU'RE BOTH *DEAD.*

JOE BOB

SKULL EATER

YOU ARE A -sniff- GOOD FRIEND, PERCY.

C'MON, BIG GUY. LET'S GET TO CLASS.

SMACK!

HEY! THE GAME HASN'T EVEN *STARTED* YET!

MY BAD.

COACH, CAN WE START THE GAME?

HMM?

OH, SURE. YOU BOYS PLAY NICE, NOW.

HUH? WHAT DO YOU MEAN--

MOTHER ALWAYS SAID WE SHOULD PLAY WITH OUR FOOD.

--F-F-FOOD?

TAKE *THAT*, BULLY!

TYSON?

FOOSH

fump

YOU MAY HAVE DISPATCHED MY BROTHERS,

BUT I'M HAPPY TO FEAST ON YOU ALONE, SON OF THE SEA GOD!

I'LL SAVE YOU!

WHAM

TYSON!

YOU LOSE, PERSEUS JACKSON.

-:HRK:-

AW, NU--

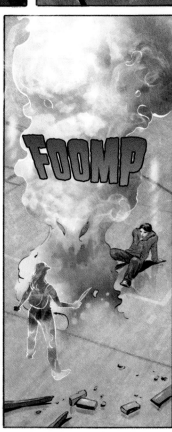

FOOMP

WHERE'D YOU FIND THAT *THING*?

TYSON? I KNOW HIM FROM SCHOOL.

YOU COULD BE NICE TO HIM. HE *SAVED MY LIFE* BACK THERE.

I BET. I'M SURPRISED THE *LAISTRYGONIANS* HAD THE GUTS TO ATTACK YOU WITH HIM AROUND.

LAISTRY-*WHAT*?

LAISTRYGONIANS. THEY'RE *CANNIBAL GIANTS* FROM THE NORTH. I'VE NEVER SEEN THEM AS FAR SOUTH AS NEW YORK. SOMETHING IS *DEFINITELY* UP.

ANNABETH... WHAT ARE YOU DOING HERE?

WHAT DO YOU THINK, *SEAWEED BRAIN*? I'VE HAD MONSTERS ON MY TAIL EVER SINCE I LEFT VIRGINIA.

I'M TRYING TO GET TO CAMP, AND I FIGURED YOU'D BE HEADING THAT WAY, TOO.

YOU KNOW, BECAUSE OF *THE DREAMS*.

I'M NOT SURE YET. WHAT HAVE *YOU* BEEN DREAMING ABOUT?

CAMP. *BIG TROUBLE* AT CAMP. I DON'T KNOW WHAT EXACTLY, BUT I KNOW THEY NEED OUR HELP.

I COULD'VE SWORN I HAD ONE DRACHMA LEFT.

THE DREAMS ABOUT GROVER?

GROVER? WHAT'S WRONG WITH GROVER?

BULLY IN THE GYM CALLED PERCY SOMETHING... "SON OF THE SEA GOD"?

OH, UH, RIGHT.

OKAY, LISTEN: YOU EVER HEAR THOSE STORIES ABOUT THE GREEK GODS? ZEUS, POSEIDON, ATHENA...?

YES.

GOT IT!

STÊTHI, Ô HÁRMA DIABOLÉS!

WELL, THOSE GODS ARE STILL ALIVE, AND SOMETIMES THEY HAVE KIDS WITH REGULAR PEOPLE. KIDS CALLED *HALF-BLOODS*.

MY DAD IS POSEIDON. THE SEA GOD.

BUT IF *YOU* ARE SON OF THE SEA GOD, THEN THAT MEANS--

SKRCH

YOU...UH...WANT YOUR EYE? THEN TELL ME ABOUT "THE LOCATION." WHAT LOCATION?

I DON'T... FEEL SO GOOD.

NO! DON'T TELL!

REMEMBER WHAT HAPPENED *LAST TIME* WE TOLD? HORRIBLE!

PERCY, ARE YOU *CRAZY?!* IF THEY CAN'T SEE, THEY'LL KEEP SPEEDING UP UNTIL WE FLY APART.

GIVE THEM THE EYE!

NOT UNTIL THEY TELL US THE LOCATION!

30, 31, 75, 12! THAT'S ALL WE CAN SAY!

NOW *GIVE US THE EYE!*

SQUISH

BRAKE!!!

SKRCH!

BORDER PATROL, TO ME!

HOLD THE LINE!

WHOOSH

RETREAT!

GET **BACK** IN FORMATION, ALL OF YOU!

WATCH OUT!

϶ooft

CURSE YOU, JACKSON! THIS IS *MY* FIGHT!

NICE TO SEE YOU, TOO, CLARISSE.

HEY, ELSIE! OVER HERE!

CRUNCH

PERCY!
RUN!

PERCY
NEEDS HELP!

BIG GUY?

I THOUGHT YOU GOT LUCKY SURVIVING THE GIANTS, BUT THAT BULL *TORCHED* YOU.

HOW...?

YOU MEAN YOU NEVER NOTICED?

NO WONDER YOU GOT AMBUSHED IN THE GYM. YOU STILL HAVEN'T LEARNED HOW TO SEE THROUGH THE *MIST*.

TAKE A *GOOD LOOK* AT TYSON. HE'S NOT A KID--

--HE'S A *CYCLOPS*.

~sniff~

HE'S JUST A BABY, BY THE LOOKS OF HIM.

PROBABLY ONE OF THE HOMELESS ORPHANS.

ONE OF WHAT?

THEY'RE *MISTAKES.*

CHILDREN OF NATURE SPIRITS AND GODS.

WELL, USUALLY *ONE GOD* IN PARTICULAR...

THEY DON'T ALWAYS COME OUT RIGHT, SO THEY GET ABANDONED TO GROW UP WILD ON THE STREETS.

OUT IN THE REAL WORLD, MIST MADE HIM LOOK LIKE ANY OTHER KID. JUST, YOU KNOW, *BIGGER.* BUT THE MIST DISSIPATED ONCE HE GOT TO CAMP.

ANYWAY, THAT'S HOW HE DEFEATED THE GIANTS AND THE BULLS. CYCLOPES ARE IMMUNE TO FIRE. THEY WORK THE FORGES OF THE GODS, SO IT'S KIND OF A PREREQUISITE.

I GUESS THAT EXPLAINS YOUR "A" IN SHOP CLASS, HM?

JACKSON!

DON'T YOU *EVER* INTERFERE WITH ONE OF MY BATTLE PLANS AGAIN.

BATTLE PLAN?

NEXT TIME YOU USE MONSTERS FOR PRACTICE, CLARISSE, TRY SUMMONING ONES YOU CAN ACTUALLY BEAT.

THAT WASN'T PRACTICE, *PUNK,* AND I DIDN'T SUMMON THEM.

THEY CROSSED THE CAMP'S BORDER ALL ON THEIR OWN.

NICE TRY, CLARISSE, BUT WE KNOW BETTER.

THE MAGIC FROM THALIA'S TREE KEEPS THE MONSTERS OUT.

YOU'VE BEEN AWAY FROM CAMP TOO LONG, MISS PRINCESS. YOU NEED TO CATCH UP ON *CURRENT EVENTS*.

OH, NO...

IT LOOKS LIKE IT'S... *DYING.*

SOMEONE *POISONED* IT.

I WOULDN'T TOUCH THAT IF I WERE YOU. IT'LL BURN RIGHT THROUGH YOUR SKIN.

NOW HELP ME GET THESE WOUNDED BACK TO THE BIG HOUSE.

ALL RIGHT. WE NEED TO TALK TO CHIRON ANYWAY.

CHIRON. *RIGHT.*

MAYBE YOU CAN CATCH HIM BEFORE HE LEAVES.

LEAVES?

PONY!

MY DEAR YOUNG CYCLOPS!

I AM A *CENTAUR*.

CHIRON!

IT IS GOOD TO SEE YOU, ANNABETH.

AND PERCY, MY GOODNESS. HOW THE TIME DOES FLY.

CHIRON, WHAT'S HAPPENING? CLARISSE SAID YOU WERE... LEAVING?

"FIRED" WOULD BE A MORE ACCURATE TERM, CHILD.

LORD ZEUS WAS MOST UPSET WHEN HE LEARNED THE TREE CREATED FROM THE SPIRIT OF HIS DAUGHTER HAD BEEN POISONED. *SOMEONE* HAD TO BE PUNISHED.

BUT THIS IS CRAZY! YOU COULDN'T HAVE HAD ANYTHING TO DO WITH THAT.

NEVERTHELESS, SOME IN OLYMPUS DO NOT TRUST ME NOW.

THE POISON IS SOMETHING FROM THE UNDERWORLD. SOME VENOM EVEN *I* HAVE NEVER SEEN.

IT MUST HAVE COME FROM A MONSTER *QUITE DEEP* IN THE PIT OF TARTARUS.

THEN IT'S OBVIOUS WHO'S TO BLAME.

DOESN'T ANYONE IN OLYMPUS REMEMBER THAT LAST SUMMER KRONOS TRIED TO START A CIVIL WAR BETWEEN THE GODS? THIS *HAS* TO BE HIS DOING.

PERHAPS, BUT I FEAR I AM BEING HELD RESPONSIBLE BECAUSE I DID NOT PREVENT IT, AND I CANNOT CURE IT.

THE TREE ONLY HAS A FEW WEEKS LEFT TO LIVE.

UNLESS...

UNLESS WHAT?

NO. A FOOLISH THOUGHT. ONLY *ONE SOURCE* OF MAGIC WOULD BE STRONG ENOUGH TO REVERSE THE POISON, BUT IT WAS LOST CENTURIES AGO.

WHAT IS IT? WE'LL GO FIND IT!

IF THE TREE DIES, CAMP WILL BE OVERRUN BY MONSTERS. WE CAN'T LET THAT HAPPEN!

YOU MUST NOT BE BAITED INTO HASTY ACTION, PERCY.

OR HAVE *YOU* FORGOTTEN THAT LAST SUMMER THE TITAN LORD TRIED TO TAKE YOUR LIFE?

I DID NOT WANT YOU TO COME HERE AT ALL THIS SUMMER, *STAY* HERE. TRAIN. LEARN TO FIGHT. BUT DO NOT LEAVE.

ANNABETH, I CHARGE YOU WITH KEEPING PERCY FROM HARM. REMEMBER THE PROPHECY.

RIGHT. THE *SUPER-DANGEROUS PROPHECY* THAT HAS ME IN IT, BUT THAT NO ONE WILL TELL ME ABOUT.

HOW COULD I FORGET THAT.

I'LL LOOK AFTER HIM, CHIRON. I PROMISE.

THERE IS NOTHING MORE TO SAY. PERHAPS MY NAME WILL BE CLEARED, AND I SHALL RETURN.

UNTIL THEN, I WILL VISIT WITH MY WILD KINSMEN IN THE EVERGLADES.

IT IS POSSIBLE THEY KNOW OF AN ANTIDOTE FOR THE POISON THAT I HAVE FORGOTTEN.

SWAT!

FAREWELL, CHILDREN.

REMEMBER MY WORDS, AND HEED THEM WELL.

COME ON. IT'S ALMOST TIME FOR DINNER.

LET'S GO FIND OUT WHO CHIRON'S *REPLACEMENT* IS.

WELL, MY MILLENNIUM IS COMPLETE. IF IT ISN'T PETER JOHNSON.

AND GUEST.

PERCY JACKSON, SIR.

WHATEVER.

YOU NEED TO WATCH THIS BOY. HE'S *POSEIDON'S* CHILD.

I SEE... I AM TANTALUS, ON *SPECIAL ASSIGNMENT*--

--AS THE NEW ACTIVITIES DIRECTOR UNTIL MY LORD DIONYSUS DECIDES OTHERWISE. I EXPECT YOU TO REFRAIN FROM CAUSING ANY TROUBLE AT *MY* CAMP, PERSEUS JACKSON.

TROUBLE? *YOUR* CAMP ALREADY HAS TROUBLE.

OR DIDN'T YOU NOTICE THE BULLS WITH BAD BREATH WHO ALMOST TORCHED THIS PLACE TODAY?

YES, *ALMOST.*

AND WHAT A *TRAGEDY* THAT WOULD'VE BEEN.

CLINK!

BLASTED *FOOD!*

AH, WELL.

BELIEVE ME, OLD CHAP, WORKING AT THIS CAMP WILL BE TORTUROUS ENOUGH TO MAKE *EVEN YOU* LOSE YOUR APPETITE.

I REMEMBER NOW... YOU'RE FROM ONE OF CHIRON'S STORIES.

YOU STOLE AMBROSIA AND NECTAR FROM THE GODS TO TRY AND FIGURE OUT THE RECIPE.

WHEN THEY BANNED YOU FROM OLYMPUS, YOU BOILED UP YOUR *OWN KID* AND TRIED TO FEED HIM TO THEM.

I GUESS THE GODS DON'T LIKE *PEOPLE* ON THE MENU, BECAUSE THEY SENT YOU TO THE FIELDS OF PUNISHMENT AND CURSED YOU TO NEVER EAT OR DRINK AGAIN.

HOW MANY CENTURIES AGO WAS THAT, ANYWAY?

I'LL BE *WATCHING YOU*, PERCY JACKSON.

NOW GO TO YOUR TABLE WHILE WE DECIDE WHAT TO DO WITH THIS...*THING* YOU BROUGHT WITH YOU.

ATTENTION, EVERYONE. THERE IS AN UNFORTUNATE BIT OF HOUSEKEEPING THAT NEEDS TENDING TO.

PERCY JACKSON AND ANNABETH CHASE HAVE SEEN FIT TO BRING *THIS* HERE.

NORMALLY, I'D RELEASE THIS BEAST INTO THE WOODS AND LET YOU HUNT IT DOWN WITH TORCHES AND POINTED STICKS, BUT PERHAPS WE SHOULD GIVE IT A CHANCE TO PROVE ITSELF WORTHY OF LIVING.

ARE THERE ANY SUGGESTIONS AS TO WHICH CABIN THE BEAST SHOULD SLEEP IN?

A *CAGE* AND *FOOD DISH* WILL BE PROVIDED, OF COURSE.

COME, NOW. THE MONSTER DOESN'T SEEM ALL BAD. IT MAY EVEN BE CAPABLE OF DOING MENIAL CHORES.

SURELY *SOMEONE*--

OH! I SEE.

IT APPEARS THE MATTER HAS ALREADY RESOLVED ITSELF.

AND A *FINE* RESOLUTION IT IS.

THE ANSWER SHOULD'VE BEEN APPARENT ALL ALONG, I SUPPOSE--

--GIVEN THE *FAMILY RESEMBLANCE.*

CAN YOU HEAR ME? PERCY?

PLEASE, I DON'T HAVE THE STRENGTH TO PROJECT ANY BETTER. YOU *HAVE* TO HEAR ME!

HONEY PIE! HAS IT BEEN TWO WEEKS YET?

N-NO, DEAREST. ONLY FIVE DAYS. THAT LEAVES *TWELVE MORE* TO GO.

BAH! WEAVE FASTER! I WANT TO *SEE* UNDER THAT VEIL! ~*heh heh heh!*~

PERCY, IF YOU CAN HEAR ME, COME HELP! I'M STUCK IN SOME CAVE ON AN ISLAND.

I DON'T KNOW WHERE, EXACTLY. I WENT TO FLORIDA, AND I TURNED LEFT.

IT'S A *TRAP*, PERCY. IT'S THE REASON NO SATYR HAS EVER RETURNED FROM THE SEARCH.

ITS NATURE MAGIC IS SO STRONG, IT SMELLS JUST LIKE THE *GREAT GOD PAN*. THE SATYRS COME HERE THINKING THEY'VE FOUND PAN, AND THEY GET CAPTURED AND EATEN BY *POLYPHEMUS!*

THIS DISGUISE IS THE ONLY THING KEEPING ME ALIVE. HE'S HALF BLIND FROM SOMEONE POKING HIM IN HIS EYE, SO HE THINKS I'M A LADY CYCLOPS...AND HE, UH, WANTS TO *MARRY* ME!

I SAID I COULDN'T MARRY HIM UNTIL MY BRIDAL TRAIN WAS FINISHED, BUT SOON HE'LL REALIZE WHAT I AM--*I JUST KNOW IT*. YOU HAVE TO HURRY!

OH, AND, UM, PERCY? THIS EMPATHY LINK WAS THE ONLY WAY I COULD THINK TO CONTACT YOU. IT MEANS OUR EMOTIONS ARE LINKED NOW, SO IF *I* DIE...

WELL, YOU *MIGHT* LIVE FOR YEARS IN A VEGETATIVE STATE. BUT, UH, IT'D BE A LOT BETTER IF YOU RESCUED ME BEFORE THAT HAPPENS.

HONEY PIE! DINNERTIME!

YUMMY YUMMY *SHEEP MEAT!*

I HAVE TO GO!

SWEET DREAMS, PERCY. *DON'T LET ME DIE!*

IT'S A NEW DAY, CAMPERS, THE FIRST FULL DAY OF MY TENURE AS ACTIVITIES DIRECTOR. I SUPPOSE I COULD EASE THE TRANSITION, BUT LET'S JUST *RIP THE BANDAGE OFF QUICKLY*, SHALL WE?

THERE ARE GOING TO BE MANY CHANGES AROUND HERE OVER THE SUMMER, BUT TO COMMEMORATE THE START OF THIS YEAR'S SESSION, I HAVE DECIDED TO REINSTATE THE *CHARIOT RACES.*

NOW, I REALIZE THAT THESE RACES WERE DISCONTINUED SOME YEARS AGO DUE TO, AH, *TECHNICAL PROBLEMS*--

THREE DEATHS AND TWENTY-SIX MUTILATIONS!

--BUT I KNOW YOU WILL ALL JOIN ME IN WELCOMING THE RETURN OF THIS CAMP TRADITION.

I'VE HAD THE OLD CHARIOTS BROUGHT OUT FROM STORAGE.

EACH CABIN WILL FIELD A TEAM CONSISTING OF A DRIVER AND A FIGHTER.

CLATTER

ROLL!

WEAPONS ARE ALLOWED, AND DIRTY TRICKS ARE EXPECTED.

BUT ANY KILLING WILL RESULT IN *HARSH PUNISHMENT:* NO S'MORES AT THE CAMPFIRE FOR A WEEK!

YOU HAVE FIVE MINUTES TO CHOOSE YOUR TEAMS AND REPORT TO THE STARTING LINE.

THERE ARE ONLY TWO OF US, SO IT LOOKS LIKE WE HAVE TO BE THE TEAM.

DON'T WORRY, THOUGH. POSEIDON *INVENTED* HORSES, SO WE'LL BE OKAY.

I TRUST YOU, PERCY.

HEY, JACKSON! MAKE SURE YOU KEEP YOUR EYE ON THE TRACK.

OH, I'M SORRY. -snicker- I MEANT *EYES.*

YOU ARE MAD BECAUSE I AM A MONSTER.

IT IS OKAY. I WILL BE A *GOOD* MONSTER. THEN YOU WILL NOT HAVE TO BE MAD.

I'M NOT MAD AT YOU. I'M MAD AT POSEIDON.

I FEEL LIKE HE'S TRYING TO *EMBARRASS* ME--LIKE HE'S TRYING TO COMPARE US OR SOMETHING--AND I DON'T UNDERSTAND WHY.

PLUS, I'M WORRIED ABOUT CAMP. AND MY FRIEND GROVER...

CHARIOTEERS! TO THE STARTING LINE!

LET'S JUST GO.

RELEASE!

FWING

READY THE CHAINS!

WHACK!

WAY TO GO, BIG GUY!

BIG GUY?

B-B-B-

AH!

SHOO, BIRDIE!

HANG ON! WE HAVE TO HELP THE OTHERS!

WHOA!

FOOMP

FOOMP

THEY'RE EVERYWHERE!

FWEET

TWEET

SQUAWK!

FWE-EET

SQUAWK!

FWEET

SQUAWK!

SQUAWK!

SQUAWK!

FWEET!

STYMPHALIAN BIRDS. THEY *HATE* NOISE.

HERCULES SCARED THEM OFF WITH BIG BRASS BELLS, BUT I DIDN'T SEE ANY OF THOSE LYING AROUND.

GROUND *AND* AIR ASSAULTS? THALIA'S TREE IS GETTING WEAKER BY THE DAY...

toot toot

BRAVO, CAMPERS!

A REMARKABLE DEMONSTRATION OF SKILL INDEED!

LET US ALL *CONGRATULATE* CLARISSE FOR WINNING THE INAUGURAL CHARIOT RACE!

THE CHARIOT RACE?

WE JUST GOT DIVE-BOMBED BY *DEMON PIGEONS*, AND YOU'RE TALKING ABOUT THE *CHARIOT RACE?*

CAUTION, LITTLE GIRL.

OR WOULD YOU LIKE TO SEE WHAT HAPPENED TO THE *LAST CHILD* WHO TESTED ME?

THE CAMP'S BORDERS ARE FAILING. IF WE DON'T DO SOMETHING TO HEAL THALIA'S TREE, WE'RE ALL DONE FOR.

NATURE MAGIC...

~hmph~ DON'T BE ABSURD.

CURING THE POISON WOULD REQUIRE A SOURCE OF NATURE MAGIC THAT IS NOT EASILY COME BY.

ANNABETH! REMEMBER THE DREAM I HAD ABOUT GROVER? WELL, I HAD ANOTHER ONE LAST NIGHT.

THIS ONE WAS DIFFERENT, THOUGH. IT WAS LIKE HE WAS TALKING TO ME.

HE SAID IT WAS AN "EMPATHY LINK." HE WAS WEARING A WEDDING DRESS, TOO, BUT THAT'S BESIDE THE POINT.

WHAT IS THE POINT?

THE POINT IS, HE SAID HE WAS TRAPPED ON AN ISLAND SOMEWHERE...

THAT THERE WAS SOME SOURCE OF NATURE MAGIC SO STRONG, HE'D MISTAKEN IT FOR PAN.

IT CAN'T BE...

PERCY, WHAT ELSE DID HE TELL YOU? THINK!

JUST THAT HE'S BEING HELD PRISONER BY SOMEONE NAMED POLYURETHANE.

NO, THAT'S NOT RIGHT. WAS IT POLYNOMIAL? POLY-SOMETHING. POLY...

POLYPHEMUS?

BINGO!

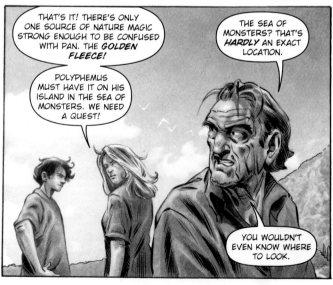

THAT'S IT! THERE'S ONLY ONE SOURCE OF NATURE MAGIC STRONG ENOUGH TO BE CONFUSED WITH PAN. THE GOLDEN FLEECE!

THE SEA OF MONSTERS? THAT'S HARDLY AN EXACT LOCATION.

POLYPHEMUS MUST HAVE IT ON HIS ISLAND IN THE SEA OF MONSTERS. WE NEED A QUEST!

YOU WOULDN'T EVEN KNOW WHERE TO LOOK.

30, 31, 75, 12.

OOO-KAY. THANKS FOR SHARING THOSE MEANINGLESS NUMBERS.

THEY'RE NOT MEANINGLESS. THE GRAY SISTERS SAID THEY KNEW THE LOCATION OF THE THING I SEEK.

THE NUMBERS ARE *SAILING COORDINATES:* 30 DEGREES, 31 MINUTES NORTH, 75 DEGREES, 12 MINUTES WEST.

THAT'S SOMEWHERE OFF THE COAST OF FLORIDA.

I'M IMPRESSED.

WHAT CAN I SAY? THE OCEAN IS IN MY BLOOD.

LISTEN, EVERYONE. THE GOLDEN FLEECE STRENGTHENS NATURE.

IT REVITALIZES ANY LAND WHERE IT'S PLACED. AND IT'LL HEAL THALIA'S TREE.

IT'S OUR *ONLY HOPE,* AND IT SOUNDS LIKE GROVER HAS FOUND IT. WE NEED A QUEST.

WE NEED A QUEST! WE NEED A QUEST!

FINE! YOU *BRATS* WANT ME TO ASSIGN A QUEST? THEN I SHALL AUTHORIZE A CHAMPION TO RETRIEVE THE GOLDEN FLEECE AND BRING IT BACK TO CAMP.

I CAN THINK OF NONE BETTER THAN THE ONE WHO HAS PROVEN HERSELF COURAGEOUS BOTH IN THE CHARIOT RACE AND IN THE BATTLE OF THE BULLS.

CLARISSE SHALL CONSULT THE ORACLE.

I ACCEPT!

CLARISSE!

CLARISSE!

WELL, THAT *ALMOST* WENT THE WAY WE WANTED IT TO.

ANY IDEAS WHAT WE SHOULD DO NOW, PERCY?

PERCY?

MAY I JOIN YOU?

I HAVEN'T SAT DOWN IN AGES.

UH, SURE...

YOUR HOSPITALITY DOES YOU CREDIT. RARELY AM I AFFORDED A MOMENT OF TRUE PEACE AND--

DEE DEE DEET

YEAH?

LISTEN, I DON'T CARE IF HE *IS* CHAINED TO A ROCK WITH VULTURES PECKING OUT HIS LIVER. IF HE DOESN'T HAVE A TRACKING NUMBER, WE CAN'T LOCATE HIS PACKAGE.

A GIFT TO HUMANKIND... NEAT. YOU KNOW HOW MANY OF *THOSE* WE DELIVER? I GOTTA GO.

THE THERMOS CONTAINS THE WINDS FROM THE FOUR CORNERS OF THE EARTH. THEY'LL HELP SPEED YOU ON YOUR WAY.

I FEEL THINNER ALREADY.

WHAT ARE YOU COMPLAINING ABOUT? MINE WAS BIGGER.

AS FOR THE MULTIVITAMINS... THEY'RE VERY POTENT. TAKE ONE ONLY IF YOU REALLY NEED IT. THEY'LL MAKE YOU FEEL LIKE YOURSELF AGAIN.

OKAY...BUT WHY ARE YOU HELPING ME? THE *LAST TIME* A GOD BROUGHT ME A GIFT, IT ALMOST GOT ME KILLED.

GOOD OLD *ARES*. FORGIVE MY BROTHER, PERCY-- HE STILL HASN'T REALIZED THAT DEATH ISN'T A VERY FUNNY PUNCH LINE.

I ASSURE YOU, THESE GIFTS COME WITH NO TRICKS ATTACHED.

LET'S JUST SAY THAT I HOPE YOUR QUEST WILL SAVE...MORE THAN YOUR FRIEND GROVER.

IF YOU'RE TALKING ABOUT LUKE, YOU CAN FORGET IT.

EVEN IF I COULD FIND HIM, I DON'T THINK HE CAN BE SAVED. HE'S BETRAYED EVERYONE HE KNOWS. HE HATES *YOU* ESPECIALLY.

MY DEAR YOUNG COUSIN, IF THERE'S ONE THING I'VE LEARNED OVER THE EONS, IT'S THAT YOU *CAN'T* GIVE UP ON FAMILY, NO MATTER HOW TEMPTING IT MAY BE.

I TOOK THE LIBERTY OF PACKING FOR YOU AND YOUR COMPANIONS. THEY WILL BE ARRIVING ANY MOMENT NOW.

IF YOU ASK NICELY, YOUR FATHER SHOULD BE ABLE TO HELP YOU REACH THE SHIP.

SHIP?

WHOOSH

PERCY!

TANTALUS ENLISTED THE CLEANING HARPIES TO ENFORCE CAMP RULES AND REGULATIONS. YOU DON'T WANT TO BE CAUGHT OUT HERE ALL BY YOURSELF.

SPECIAL DELIVERY FROM *HERMES*.

...WHAT'S WITH THIS STUFF?

APPARENTLY, HE THINKS I SHOULD BE THE ONE TO GO AFTER THE FLEECE.

THE SEARCH BEGINS WITH THAT CRUISE LINER ON THE HORIZON.

PERCY, WE *HAVE* TO TAKE THIS QUEST.

"WE"? WHAT ABOUT YOUR PROMISE TO CHIRON?

I PROMISED I'D KEEP YOU SAFE FROM DANGER.

I CAN DO THAT ONLY BY COMING WITH YOU, RIGHT?

ME, TOO!

HANG ON A MINUTE. WHERE WE'RE GOING ISN'T THE BEST PLACE FOR A CYCLOPS.

YOU CAN STAY BEHIND AND TELL THE OTHERS--

TYSON CAN COME IF HE WANTS TO.

WANT TO!

IT'S SETTLED, THEN.

YOU GUYS WAIT HERE.

UM, DAD? HOW'S IT GOING?

WE NEED TO GET TO THAT SHIP. THINK YOU CAN...HELP US OUT?

NOW *THAT'S* WHAT I CALL A RIDE.

GOOD AFTERNOON, PASSENGERS. WE'LL BE AT SEA ALL DAY TODAY.

EXCELLENT WEATHER FOR THE POOLSIDE MAMBO PARTY. DON'T FORGET MILLION-DOLLAR BINGO IN THE KRAKEN LOUNGE, AND FOR OUR **SPECIAL GUESTS**, DISEMBOWELING PRACTICE ON THE PROMENADE.

DID HE JUST SAY "DISEMBOWELING PRACTICE"?

WE ARE ON A CRUISE. WE ARE HAVING FUN.

WE ARE ON A CRUISE. WE ARE HAVING FUN.

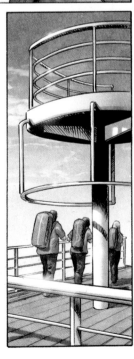

WE ARE ON A CRUISE.

WE ARE HAVING FUN.

WE ARE ON A CRUISE. WE ARE HAVING FUN.

RRRRRR

THIS IS *WEIRD*... THEY'RE ALL IN SOME KIND OF TRANCE.

P-PUPPY?

PERCY, IS THAT...?

LUKE!

HIDE!

IT'S ONLY A MATTER OF *TIME*. DON'T PUSH ME, AGRIUS!

I'M NOT PUSHING YOU. I'M JUST SAYING, IF THE GAMBLE DOESN'T PAY OFF--

THEY'LL TAKE THE BAIT. DON'T WORRY ABOUT THAT.

LET'S GET TO THE ADMIRALTY SUITE AND CHECK ON THE CASKET.

LEAVE NOW?

NOT UNTIL WE FIND OUT WHAT LUKE IS UP TO.

I CAN'T HEAR A THING. THE DOORS MUST BE TOO THICK!

"YOU REALLY THINK THE OLD HORSEMAN IS DONE FOR GOOD?"

"THEY CAN'T TRUST HIM. NOT WITH THE SKELETONS IN *HIS* CLOSET. THE POISONING OF THE TREE WAS THE FINAL STRAW."

HOW'RE YOU DOING THAT, TYSON? YOU SOUND JUST LIKE *LUKE*.

SHH!

TYSON, WHAT ELSE ARE THEY SAYING?

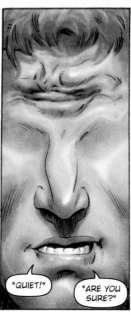

"QUIET!"

"ARE YOU SURE?"

"YES. RIGHT OUTSIDE."

UH, GUYS? MAYBE WE SHOULD--

WELL, IF IT ISN'T MY TWO FAVORITE COUSINS.

--RUN?

MY NEW PAD IS A BIT NICER THAN *CABIN ELEVEN*, DON'T YOU THINK?

I HOPE YOU APPRECIATE US LETTING YOU SURVIVE FOR ANOTHER YEAR, PERCY. HOW'S YOUR MOM? HOW'S SCHOOL?

YOU POISONED THALIA'S TREE.

SURE, I POISONED THE TREE. SO WHAT? IF YOU KNEW WHAT WAS COMING, YOU'D UNDERSTAND.

I UNDERSTAND YOU WANT TO DESTROY THE CAMP. BUT HOW COULD YOU?

THALIA SAVED OUR LIVES. *YOUR* LIFE!

THE GODS HAVE BLINDED YOU, ANNABETH. YOU CAN'T EVEN IMAGINE A WORLD WITHOUT THEM.

HALF-BLOOD HILL WILL BE OVERRUN WITH MONSTERS WITHIN A MONTH. THE HEROES WHO SURVIVE WILL HAVE NO CHOICE BUT TO JOIN US OR BE HUNTED TO EXTINCTION.

THE WEST IS *ROTTEN* TO THE CORE. IT HAS TO BE DESTROYED.

YOUR HOPELESS QUEST TO FIND THE FLEECE WON'T CHANGE A THING.

DON'T LOOK SO SURPRISED. I KNOW ALL ABOUT YOUR PLANS. I STILL HAVE FRIENDS AT CAMP WHO KEEP ME POSTED.

SPIES, YOU MEAN.

THE GODS ARE *SO* USING YOU, PERCY. DO YOU KNOW WHAT'S IN STORE FOR YOU IF YOU REACH YOUR SIXTEENTH BIRTHDAY?

HAS CHIRON EVEN TOLD YOU THE PROPHECY?

LUKE, LISTEN TO ME. *YOUR FATHER* SENT US.

HE TOLD ME HE WON'T GIVE UP ON YOU, NO MATTER HOW ANGRY YOU ARE.

GIVE UP ON ME? HE ABANDONED ME!

I WANT OLYMPUS DESTROYED! YOU TELL HERMES IT'S GOING TO HAPPEN, TOO.

EACH TIME A HALF-BLOOD JOINS US, THE OLYMPIANS GROW WEAKER. AND *KRONOS* GROWS STRONGER.

LITTLE BY LITTLE, WE'RE CALLING HIS LIFE FORCE OUT OF THE PIT. WITH EVERY NEW RECRUIT, ANOTHER SMALL PIECE APPEARS...

GO TO HADES.

YOU FIRST.

ORIEUS, HAVE SECURITY TAKE OUR STOWAWAYS BELOWDECKS TO MEET THE AETHIOPIAN DRAKON. I BELIEVE IT'S *FEEDING TIME.*

AGRIUS, YOU STAY HERE WITH ME. WE HAVE IMPORTANT MATTERS TO DISCUSS.

TYSON! NOW!

GO AWAY!

~grnt~

RANGALANGALANG

THE ALARM!

ANGALANGALANGA

GET TO THE LIFEBOAT!

WHAT'S TAKING SO LONG?!?

IT'S *STUCK*! I CAN'T LAUNCH IT!

WHAM!

HOLD ON TO SOMETHING!

SHWIP

LATER.

WE SURE GOT OUT OF THERE IN A HURRY. OF COURSE, NOW WE HAVE *NO IDEA* WHERE WE ARE...

36 DEGREES, 44 MINUTES NORTH, 76 DEGREES, 2 MINUTES WEST. JUST OFF THE COAST OF VIRGINIA BEACH.

WHOA. HOW DID I KNOW THAT?

BECAUSE OF YOUR DAD. WHEN YOU'RE AT SEA, YOU HAVE PERFECT BEARINGS. THAT IS *SO* COOL.

HEY. I'M SORRY ABOUT, YOU KNOW...SEEING *LUKE.*

IT'S NOT YOUR FAULT. HE MADE HIS DECISION.

BUT I'M WORRIED OUR ESCAPE WAS A LITTLE TOO EASY. HE SAID SOMETHING ABOUT A "GAMBLE" AND "THEY'LL TAKE THE BAIT." HE COULD'VE BEEN TALKING ABOUT US.

WHAT'S THE BAIT? GROVER, OR THE FLEECE?

MAYBE HE WANTS THE FLEECE FOR HIMSELF.

MAYBE HE'S HOPING WE'LL DO THE HARD WORK, AND THEN HE CAN *STEAL* IT FROM US.

OF ALL THE *DIRTY TRICKS*--

QUIET! I THINK I HEAR SOMETHING.

CHUG CHUG CHUG

CHUG CHUG CHUG

YOU THREE ARE IN *BIG* TROUBLE.

CAPTAIN, BRING THESE LOSERS ABOARD.

TANTALUS *EXPELLED* YOU FOR ETERNITY.

MR. D. SAID IF ANY OF YOU SHOW YOUR FACE AT CAMP AGAIN, HE'LL TURN YOU INTO SQUIRRELS AND RUN YOU OVER WITH HIS JEEP.

DID TANTALUS AND MR. D. GIVE YOU THIS SHIP?

THE SPIRITS ON THE LOSING SIDE OF EVERY WAR OWE A TRIBUTE TO ARES. I PRAYED TO MY DAD FOR A NAVAL TRANSPORT, AND HERE IT IS.

THE CREW WILL DO *ANYTHING* I TELL THEM.

WHERE ARE YOUR CABIN MATES? THERE ARE SUPPOSED TO BE *THREE* HEROES TO A QUEST.

THEY DIDN'T...

I LET THEM STAY BEHIND. TO PROTECT CAMP.

MORE LIKE THEY DIDN'T WANT TO HELP YOU.

TANTALUS IS USING YOU. HE'D LOVE TO SEE THE CAMP DESTROYED. HE'S SETTING YOU UP TO FAIL.

SHUT UP, PRISSY! THIS IS MY QUEST. FINALLY I GET TO BE THE HERO, AND YOU TWO WON'T STEAL MY GLORY.

YOU THREE ARE MY GUESTS FOR NOW, BUT YOU CAN JUST AS EASILY BE MY *PRISONERS*. SO I SUGGEST YOU STAY HERE UNTIL TOLD OTHERWISE.

SLEEP TIGHT, LOSERS. *MAKE SURE* THE BEDBUGS BITE.

WHUNK

TIME...

NEED MORE TIME!

HONEY PIE! WHAT ARE YOU DOING?

JUST WEAVING MY BRIDAL TRAIN, DEAREST!

TOO MANY DELAYS! ALMOST DONE?

T-TEN MORE DAYS, DEAREST.

FIVE DAYS!

SEVEN, THEN, IF YOU INSIST.

SEVEN IS LESS THAN FIVE?

OH, YES. CERTAINLY!

HMPH.

HURRY, PERCY.

PLEASE, PLEASE, PLEASE!

ALL HANDS ON DECK! ALL HANDS ON DECK!

WE'VE REACHED THE ENTRANCE TO THE SEA OF MONSTERS!

GROVER... HE'S RUNNING OUT OF TIME.

~snz-zort~

FULL STEAM AHEAD, CAPTAIN.

AYE, M'LADY.

WE'RE HERE ALREADY? HOW'D WE SAIL SO FAST?

IN CASE YOU HAVEN'T NOTICED, THIS ISN'T A *TYPICAL* SHIP.

IS THAT WHAT I THINK IT IS?

ARE YOU *NUTS*?

SCYLLA AND HER SISTER, CHARYBDIS.

YOU'RE HEADING STRAIGHT FOR THEM! WHY DON'T YOU JUST SAIL AROUND?

THEY'D JUST APPEAR IN MY PATH AGAIN.

IF YOU WANT PASSAGE INTO THE SEA OF MONSTERS, YOU *HAVE* TO SAIL THROUGH THEM.

SCYLLA IS TOO HIGH UP FOR THE CANNONS, BUT CHARYBDIS JUST SITS IN THE MIDDLE OF THAT WHIRLWIND. WE'RE GOING TO STEAM RIGHT AT HER AND BLOW HER TO TARTARUS!

READY THE CANNONS, CAPTAIN. FULL BARRAGE ON MY ORDER!

THIS ISN'T GOING TO WORK. THINK YOU CAN CONTROL THE WATER AND GUIDE US THROUGH?

AGAINST SOMETHING LIKE *THAT?* NO WAY.

TOO MUCH STRAIN ON THE PISTONS. NOT MEANT FOR DEEP WATER.

FLOOOOSH

WHAT'S HAPPENING?!

FLOOOOSH

WE'RE NOT REVERSING?! THIS IS **BAD!**

WE'RE IN THE VORTEX! **FULL REVERSE!**

BOILER ROOM OVERHEATING, M'LADY! SHE'S GOING TO BLOW!

I CAN FIX IT!

TYSON, NO! IT'S TOO DANGEROUS!

GUNS IN RANGE, M'LADY!

FIRE!

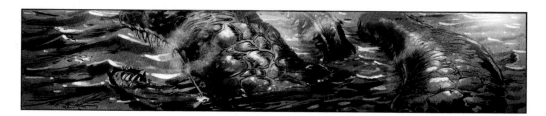

CLANG

ERRRCH

WE HAVE TO ABANDON SHIP, M'LADY. SHE'S TEARING APART!

THE BOILER CAN'T--

EVERYONE, GET BELOW!

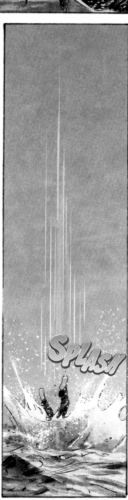

-;groan;-

GO EASY. YOU TOOK A HARD KNOCK ON THE HEAD.

TYSON...?

PERCY, I'M SO SORRY.

MAYBE HE SURVIVED THE EXPLOSION.

I MEAN...FIRE CAN'T KILL HIM.

WHAT IS THIS PLACE?

I SAILED US HERE IN ONE OF THE *BIRMINGHAM'S* LIFEBOATS. IT'S SOME KIND OF *ISLAND RESORT* OR SOMETHING.

PERHAPS *THIS* WOULD BE MORE TO YOUR LIKING?

WOW. THAT'S... AMAZING. CAN YOU REALLY--?

IT'S QUITE SIMPLE, REALLY.

JUST ONE OF OUR PATENTED *SHAKEOVERS*, SUBSTITUTED FOR A REGULAR MEAL.

I GUARANTEE YOU'LL SEE RESULTS IMMEDIATELY.

HOW IS THAT POSSIBLE?

WHY QUESTION A GOOD THING?

PERCY, THE HARDEST PART ABOUT A MAKEOVER IS GIVING UP CONTROL. YOU HAVE TO DECIDE WHOSE JUDGMENT YOU'D RATHER TRUST: *YOURS* OR *MINE*.

EXCELLENT CHOICE.

-*gak*-

CRASH!

MISS C.C.? PERCY?

KNOCK KNOCK

AH, ANNABETH! WHAT DID YOU THINK OF THE GROUNDS?

...WHERE'S PERCY?

I HELPED HIM REALIZE HIS *TRUE FORM*. BUT NEVER MIND HIM. STRONG WOMEN LIKE US DON'T NEED MEN.

LIKE US? YOU MEAN...YOU KNOW WHO I AM?

OF COURSE. I KNOW A DAUGHTER OF ATHENA WHEN I SEE ONE.

WE ARE NOT SO DIFFERENT, YOU AND I. WE BOTH SEEK KNOWLEDGE. WE BOTH ADMIRE GREATNESS.

AND LIKE ME, YOU HAVE THE MAKINGS OF A *SORCERESS*.

SORCERESS? YOU'RE...C.C....CIRCE!

THAT'S RIGHT, MY DEAR. MY MOTHER IS HECATE, THE GODDESS OF MAGIC. STAY WITH ME, AND I WILL TEACH YOU THE WAYS OF SORCERY.

FOR WOMEN, MAGIC IS THE ONLY WAY TO ACHIEVE POWER.

AS FOR YOUR FRIEND...

HE WILL BE WELL CARED FOR ON THE MAINLAND. THERE IS ALWAYS A KINDERGARTEN LOOKING FOR A NEW *CLASS PET*.

REET! REET!

SO, WHAT IS YOUR ANSWER?

THIS!

REALLY? A KNIFE AGAINST *MY MAGIC*? IS THAT WISE?

PERHAPS YOU'LL LEARN SOME MANNERS AFTER I'VE TURNED YOU INTO A SHREW!

CRACKLE

IMPOSSIBLE... HOW...?

SHAKE SHAKE

CURSE HERMES AND HIS MULTIVITAMINS! THEY'LL ONLY PROTECT YOU FOR A LITTLE WHILE; YOU'LL SEE.

A LITTLE WHILE IS *ALL THE TIME* I NEED.

NO! DON'T!

REET!

nibble

nibble

nibble

POOF!

SEAWEED BRAIN, WE'D NEED A CREW OF, LIKE, A *BAZILLION* TO GET THIS SHIP UNDER WAY!

MIZZENMAST!

MIZZEN*WHAT*?!

SHW*IP*

WHRRR

HOW DID YOU...?

DO YOU *REALLY* NEED TO ASK?

IS IT TOO MUCH TO ASK THAT I HAVE A NORMAL DREAM FOR ONCE?

THIS ONE WAS ABOUT SOME SPIKY-HAIRED GIRL WHO WANTED ME TO OPEN KRONOS'S COFFIN. WHATEVER *THAT* MEANS.

ANNABETH? *HELLO-O.*

WE'RE APPROACHING THE ISLAND OF THE SIRENS.

~*yawn*~
NO BIG DEAL. I'LL JUST HAVE THE SHIP SAIL AROUND IT.

ALL WE HAVE TO DO IS STAY OUT OF EARSHOT, RIGHT?

NO. YOU'RE GOING TO TIE ME UP AND SAIL STRAIGHT FOR IT.

I WANT TO HEAR THEM SING.

YOU *WHAT?!*

HAVE YOU FORGOTTEN THE STORIES? YOU KNOW, THE ONES WHERE THE SIRENS ENCHANT SAILORS AND LURE THEM TO THEIR *DEATHS*?

PERCY, THEY SAY THE SIRENS SING ABOUT YOUR DESIRES. THEY SHOW YOU THINGS ABOUT YOURSELF THAT EVEN YOU DON'T KNOW. THAT'S WHAT'S SO ENCHANTING.

IF YOU SURVIVE... YOU BECOME WISER. I DON'T WANT TO MISS THAT CHANCE.

PLEASE?

THIS IS NUTS...

NO MATTER HOW MUCH I BEG, DON'T UNTIE ME. I'LL GO STRAIGHT OVERBOARD AND DROWN MYSELF.

AND DON'T FORGET TO PLUG YOUR EARS.

"WE MADE IT TO POLYPHEMUS'S ISLAND."

CLATTER

MY BAD.

ϡɾnfϡ GLAD TO HELP.

~whew~

~ohhh~

GARRR!

MOVE ALONG, LITTLE SHEEPIES!

ATTABOY, BELTBUSTER... THERE YOU GO, TAMMANY...

THE BOTTOM BRANCH OF THAT TREE. LOOK.

IT'S *THE FLEECE*. YOU THINK WE CAN SWIPE IT WHILE POLYPHEMUS IS GRAZING HIS SHEEP?

MAYBE. BUT WE NEED TO RESCUE GROVER FIRST.

COME ON. LET'S GO OPEN THE CAVE.

LATER.

MUCH LATER.

WE ⇥huff⇤ NEED A NEW PLAN ⇥huff⇤.

AND I HAVE JUST THE IDEA.

TELL ME, HOW MUCH DO YOU LIKE SHEEP?

GROVER!
WHERE ARE
YOU?

OVER
HERE!

PERCY! I *KNEW* THE
EMPATHY LINK WENT
THROUGH!

GROVER,
WE NEED TO--

CLARISSE?
WHAT ARE *YOU*
DOING HERE?

THIS IS
MY QUEST,
PUNK.

I ROWED ONE OF
THE *BIRMINGHAM'S*
LIFEBOATS HERE SO
I COULD FINISH
THE JOB.

THAT'S WHEN I
DISCOVERED HORN-
HEAD GETTING READY
FOR HIS CYCLOPS
WEDDING.

I HAD
POLYPHEMUS CONVINCED
I WAS A LADY CYCLOPS, BUT
YOU BLEW MY COVER.

HMPH. I DID YOU A
FAVOR, IF YOU ASK ME.
NOW HE ONLY WANTS
TO *EAT* YOU.

IT'S *ME*
THAT HE WANTS
TO MARRY.

WHAT ABOUT TYSON?
WAS ANYONE ELSE ON BOARD
YOUR LIFEBOAT?

JUST ME. EVERYONE ELSE...
WELL, I DIDN'T EVEN KNOW
YOU MADE IT OUT.

GUYS?
MAYBE WE SHOULD
GET REACQUAINTED
AFTER WE'VE LEFT
THE ISLAND...?

BAD POLYPHEMUS!

NOT ALL CYCLOPES ARE AS NICE AS WE LOOK!

BIG GUY!

YOU'RE *ALIVE!* HOW?

FISH PONIES FOUND ME. WE'VE BEEN SWIMMING AROUND LOOKING FOR YOU. WHEN I SMELLED LOTS OF SHEEP, I CAME HERE.

GUYS... ANNABETH'S HURT...

I DON'T THINK SHE'S GOING TO MAKE IT.

WHAT HAPPENED?

WHY ARE YOU LOOKING AT ME LIKE THAT, SEAWEED BRAIN?

BECAUSE I'M GLAD YOU'RE NOT DEAD.

HOW DO YOU FEEL? CAN YOU MOVE?

RARRRRRR

WATCH ME.

HI, RAINBOW. YOU MISS ME?

NOT NOW, TYSON!

I'LL GET YOU, NOBODY!

SPLASH

TAKE US TO THE MAINLAND, FAST AS YOU CAN!

THE ISLAND... WHAT'S HAPPENING TO IT?

WITHOUT THE FLEECE'S MAGIC, IT'S REVERTING TO ITS NATURAL STATE.

I JUST HOPE THE MAGIC IS STRONG ENOUGH TO *SAVE CAMP...*

MIAMI BEACH.

JUNE 18TH! WE'VE BEEN GONE FROM CAMP TEN DAYS.

THALIA'S TREE MUST BE ALMOST DEAD.

WE HAVE TO GET THE FLEECE BACK. *TONIGHT*.

YEAH, RIGHT. WE'RE HUNDREDS OF MILES AWAY, AND WE DON'T HAVE A RIDE. THIS IS JUST LIKE *THE ORACLE* SAID.

CLARISSE...WHAT EXACTLY DID THE ORACLE TELL YOU?

YOU SHALL SAIL THE IRON SHIP WITH WARRIORS OF BONE, YOU SHALL FIND WHAT YOU SEEK AND MAKE IT YOUR OWN--

--BUT DESPAIR FOR YOUR LIFE ENTOMBED WITHIN STONE, AND FAIL WITHOUT FRIENDS, TO FLY HOME ALONE.

OUCH...

NO, WAIT... I THINK I'VE GOT IT.

EVERYBODY POOL THEIR CASH TOGETHER.

NO CASH. ALL I HAVE IS THIS GREEN PAPER.

DID YOU ROB A BANK WHEN I WASN'T LOOKING?

IT WAS IN MY YELLOW DUFFEL BAG. I THOUGHT IT WAS A TREAT FOR RAINBOW.

CLARISSE, TAKE THE MONEY AND THE FLEECE. YOU'RE GOING TO THE AIRPORT.

YOU'D LET ME--?

YEAH, YOU'D LET *HER*?

IT'S YOUR QUEST, AND WE ONLY HAVE ENOUGH MONEY FOR ONE FLIGHT. THAT'S WHAT THE ORACLE'S PROPHECY MEANT: YOU WOULDN'T GET THE FLEECE WITHOUT OUR HELP, BUT YOU'D HAVE TO FLY HOME ALONE.

YOU CAN COUNT ON ME. I WON'T FAIL.

NOT FAILING WOULD BE GOOD.

YOU REALIZE YOU'RE BETTING THE LIVES OF EVERYONE AT CAMP THAT CLARISSE WILL GET THE FLEECE BACK IN TIME.

HOW WOULD YOU FEEL IF A BUNCH OF HEROES BUTTED IN ON *YOUR* QUEST AND SHOWED YOU UP?

SHE DESERVES A CHANCE.

NOW COME ON, LET'S FIND ANOTHER WAY--

--HOME?

HEY, CUZ. WELCOME BACK TO THE STATES.

WELCOME ABOARD, TWERPS.

THE FLEECE. WHERE IS IT?

YOU'VE BEEN TOYING WITH US ALL ALONG. YOU *LET US* ESCAPE LAST TIME SO WE'D DO ALL THE HARD WORK AND GET THE FLEECE FOR YOU.

I'M NOT *ALL BAD*, PERCY. I WAS GOING TO LET YOU HAVE THE FLEECE ONCE I WAS DONE WITH IT.

DONE HEALING KRONOS, YOU MEAN.

TOO BAD WE ALREADY SENT THE FLEECE BACK TO CAMP.

LOOKS LIKE YOU *MESSED UP*. HOW'S YOUR BOSS GOING TO LIKE THAT?

SO, YOU SENT CLARISSE AHEAD WITH THE FLEECE. I DIDN'T EXPECT THAT.

IT'S TRUE, THE FLEECE'S MAGIC WOULD SPEED UP KRONOS'S HEALING BY TENFOLD.

BUT MAKE NO MISTAKE--HE *IS* STILL HEALING. YOU HAVEN'T STOPPED US. YOU'VE ONLY SLOWED US DOWN A LITTLE.

AND YOU'VE GIVEN ME AN EXCUSE TO KILL YOU. YOU'RE AN UNRELIABLE WEAPON, PERCY, AND YOU NEED TO BE REPLACED.

IT'S TIME I FORMALLY INTRODUCED YOU TO *BACKBITER*. HALF CELESTIAL BRONZE AND HALF STEEL, THE BLADE WORKS ON MORTALS *AND* IMMORTALS.

SINCE YOU'RE A LITTLE BIT OF BOTH, THAT MEANS I GET TO KILL YOU *TWICE*.

YOU AND ME, LUKE. ONE ON ONE.

YOU READ MY MIND. I'LL KILL YOU *QUICKLY*, THOUGH. THEN I'M GOING TO CHASE DOWN CLARISSE.

WHAT, NO SHIELD? *tsk-tsk.*

YOU *REALLY* SHOULD'VE COME MORE PREPARED!

SLICE

CLANG

MY, PERCY. YOU'RE OUT OF PRACTICE.

AAH!

I WANT YOU TO SEE SOMETHING BEFORE YOU DIE, PERCY.

ORIEUS, YOU CAN EAT YOUR MEAL NOW. *BON APPETIT.*

-:CHIK:-

THUNK

ATTACK, YOU FOOLS!

WHUMP

POP

POP

POP

BRETHREN, RETRIEVE *THE CAMPERS!*

QUICKLY, CHILD! LUKE'S FORCES WON'T BE DISORIENTED FOR LONG!

DUDE! ~groan~ DO THE WORDS "LOW-CARB DIET" MEAN ANYTHING TO YOU?

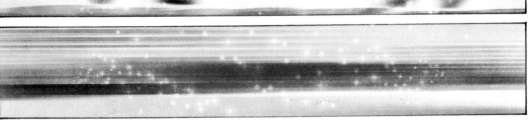

SO, AS YOU CAN SEE, CHIRON DIDN'T HAVE ANYTHING TO DO WITH POISONING THALIA'S TREE. *LUKE* DID IT SO HE COULD BRING HIS SHIP HERE AND ATTACK CAMP.

BRAVO, PETER JOHNSON.

I SUPPOSE NOW I SHALL HAVE TO REINSTATE CHIRON AS ACTIVITIES DIRECTOR. OH, HOW I'VE MISSED OUR *TEDIOUS* CARD GAMES.

I-I GOT IT! AFTER ALL THESE MILLENNIA, *I GOT IT!*

BULLY FOR YOU.

THE CAMP IS NO LONGER IN NEED OF YOUR SERVICES, TANTALUS.

YOU MAY RETURN TO THE UNDERWORLD NOW.

WHAT? BUT, *NO*--

POOF

EAT *THAT*, JERK!

WOO-HOO!

ALL RIGHT!

MR. D., PERHAPS NOW WOULD BE A GOOD TIME TO HAVE THE FLEECE BROUGHT TO THE TREE? THE *SOONER* THE HEALING PROCESS BEGINS...

VERY WELL. CLARISSE, YOU MAY HAVE THE HONORS.

SHOULD ANYONE NEED ME, I'LL BE AT THE BIG HOUSE, REMINISCING OVER HOW CLOSE I WAS TO BEING RID OF THIS *BLASTED CAMP* FOREVER.

CLARISSE! CLARISSE!

PERCY, REMAIN WITH ME A MOMENT.

THERE ARE SOME MATTERS WE MUST DISCUSS.

WHY THE LONG FACE, CHIRON? WE BROUGHT THE FLEECE BACK, SO THE CAMP'S BORDERS WILL BE RESTORED.

WE WON, RIGHT?

I'M AFRAID TODAY WAS SOMETHING OF A DRAW. WE DIDN'T HAVE THE NUMBERS TO TAKE THAT SHIP, AND LUKE WASN'T ORGANIZED ENOUGH TO PURSUE US.

BUT WITH KRONOS'S HELP, HE *WILL GET* ORGANIZED. AND BOTH SIDES WILL UNDOUBTEDLY CROSS SWORDS AGAIN.

IT HAS ALL BEEN FORETOLD.

FORETOLD?

YOU'VE BEEN GIVEN A PROPHECY FROM THE ORACLE?

INDEED. I WAS WARNED ABOUT A HALF-BLOOD CHILD SIRED BY ONE OF THE *BIG THREE*--ZEUS, POSEIDON, OR HADES. THE NEXT OF THEIR CHILDREN WHO REACHES THE AGE OF SIXTEEN WILL BE A DANGEROUS WEAPON.

HE OR SHE WILL MAKE A DECISION THAT EITHER *SAVES* THE WEST, OR *DESTROYS* IT.

WHEN I FIRST LEARNED OF THALIA, I ASSUMED SHE WAS THE CHILD THE ORACLE SPOKE OF. THAT IS WHY I TRIED SO DESPERATELY TO HAVE HER BROUGHT SAFELY TO CAMP.

WHEN SHE DIED, I HAD NO IDEA WHAT TO THINK. THEN *YOU* ARRIVED...

THIS CHILD OF THE BIG THREE...COULDN'T IT BE, LIKE, A CYCLOPS OR SOMETHING?

THE PROPHECY WAS VERY SPECIFIC. IT SAID "HALF-BLOOD." THAT REFERS ONLY TO A CHILD OF *HUMAN* AND *DIVINE* LINEAGE.

IS IT ME? AM I THE KID IN THE PROPHECY?

I WISH I KNEW. YOU WILL NOT BE SIXTEEN FOR THREE MORE YEARS, THOUGH, AND THREE YEARS CAN BE AN ETERNITY FOR A HALF-BLOOD.

FOR NOW WE MUST SIMPLY TRAIN YOU AS BEST WE CAN, AND LEAVE THE FUTURE TO THE FATES.

AND IN THE MEANTIME, KRONOS KEEPS GETTING STRONGER.

I'M JUST A *KID*, CHIRON. WHAT GOOD IS ONE LOUSY HERO AGAINST SOMETHING LIKE KRONOS?

"WHAT GOOD IS ONE LOUSY HERO?" JOSHUA LAWRENCE CHAMBERLAIN SAID THAT TO ME JUST BEFORE HE CHANGED THE COURSE OF THE AMERICAN CIVIL WAR.

YOU ARE PART HUMAN, PART GOD. YOU LIVE IN BOTH WORLDS, PERCY, AND YOU CAN AFFECT BOTH. THAT IS WHAT MAKES HALF-BLOODS SO SPECIAL. YOU CARRY THE HOPES OF HUMANITY INTO THE REALM OF THE ETERNAL. DO YOU UNDERSTAND?

I...I DON'T KNOW.

YOU MUST TRY. BECAUSE WHETHER OR NOT YOU ARE THE CHILD OF THE PROPHECY, KRONOS THINKS YOU MAY BE. AND AFTER TODAY, HE WILL FINALLY DESPAIR OF TURNING YOU TO HIS SIDE.

THAT *IS* THE ONLY REASON HE HASN'T KILLED YOU YET, YOU KNOW. NOW THAT HE'S SURE HE CAN'T USE YOU, HE WILL DESTROY YOU.

YOU TALK LIKE YOU KNOW HIM.

I *DO* KNOW HIM.

REMEMBER YOUR STUDY OF MYTHOLOGY. WHAT IS MY CONNECTION TO THE TITAN LORD?

YOU...UH... OWE HIM A FAVOR OR SOMETHING?

NO, PERCY. KRONOS IS MY *FATHER*.

ENOUGH TALK OF DARK THINGS.

THE FLEECE IS SETTING ABOUT ITS WORK.

THE CLOUDS HAVE PARTED. THE STRAWBERRIES ARE BLOOMING.

LET US ENJOY THIS HAPPY TIME.

CHIRON! PERCY!

ANNABETH... →huff← →huff← ON THE HILL...

SHE'S JUST... *LYING THERE.*

ALL OF A SUDDEN...THERE SHE WAS.

ANNABETH? *WHO* WAS THERE?

I SAID I KNOW THE TITAN LORD, BUT APPARENTLY I DO NOT KNOW HIM WELL ENOUGH. TODAY HE HAS TRULY EARNED HIS REPUTATION AS THE CROOKED ONE.

WHAT DO YOU MEAN? WHAT'S GOING ON?

HE'S TRICKED US AGAIN. GIVEN HIMSELF ANOTHER CHANCE TO CONTROL THE PROPHECY.

THE FLEECE HEALED THE TREE, AND POISON IS NOT THE *ONLY THING* IT PURGED.

YOU. I'VE SEEN YOU BEFORE.

WHO *ARE* YOU...?

Adapted from the novel
Percy Jackson & the Olympians, Book Two: *The Sea of Monsters*

Text copyright © 2013 by Rick Riordan
Illustrations copyright © 2013 Disney Enterprises, Inc.

Design by Jim Titus

Printed in the United States of America
V381-8386-5-12001
First Edition
10 9 8 7 6 5 4 3 2 1

Library of Congress Cataloging-in-Publication Data
The sea of monsters : the graphic novel / by Rick Riordan ; adapted by Robert Venditti ;
art by Attila Futaki ; lettering by Chris Dickey.—1st ed.
p. cm.—(Percy Jackson & the Olympians ; bk. 2)
Summary: After discovering a secret that makes him question the honor of being the son of Poseidon,
demigod Percy Jackson journeys into the Sea of Monsters in an attempt to save Camp Half-Blood.
ISBN 978-1-4231-4529-5 (hardcover)—ISBN 978-1-4231-4550-9 (paperback)
1. Graphic novels. [1. Graphic novels. 2. Mythology, Greek—Fiction. 3. Monsters—Fiction.
4. Fathers and sons—Fiction. 5. Poseidon (Greek deity)—Fiction. 6. Riordan, Rick. Sea of monsters—
Adaptations.] I. Futaki, Attila, ill. II. Riordan, Rick. Sea of monsters. III. Title.
PZ7.7.V48Se 2012
741.5'973—dc23   2011012356

Visit www.PercyJacksonBooks.com
and www.disneyhyperionbooks.com